MIDLOTHIAN PUBLIC LIBRARY

W9-CTV-905

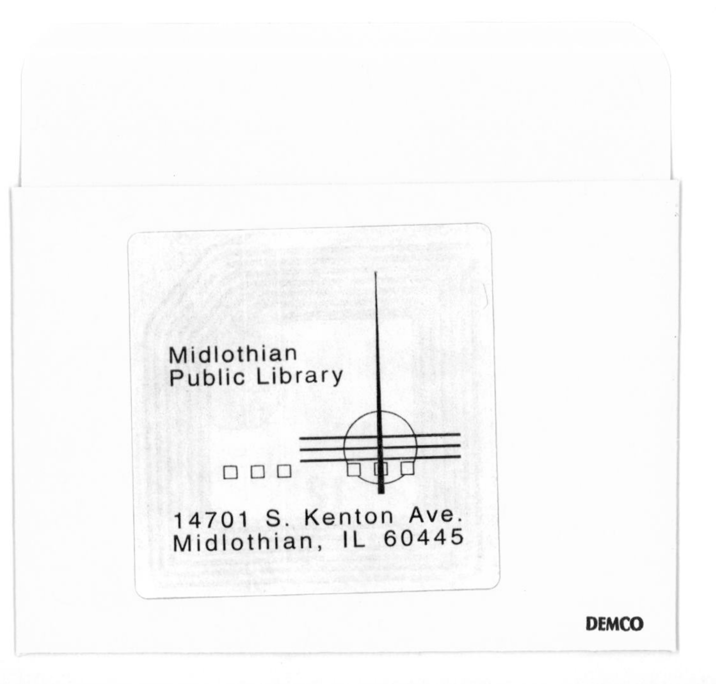
Midlothian
Public Library
14701 S. Kenton Ave.
Midlothian, IL 60445
DEMCO

SEE HOW PLANTS GROW

Vegetables

Nicola Edwards

PowerKiDS press.

New York

Published in 2008 by The Rosen Publishing Group, Inc.
29 East 21st Street, New York, NY 10010

First Edition

The publishers would like to thank the following for allowing us to reproduce their pictures in this book:
Alamy images: 20 (blickwinkel/fotototo). Corbis images: 8 (Douglas Peebles), 18 (Eric Crichton). Ecoscene: 14 (Sea Spring Photos). Garden Picture Library: 6 (David Cavagnaro), 11 (Botanica), 22 (Friedrich Strauss). Getty images: title page and 9 (Wayne Eastep), 4 (Dan Kenyon), 10 (abiggerboat, Inc), 12 (Ross M. Horowitz), 16 (Gabor Geissler), 17 (Olive Nichols), 19 (Marc O'Finley), 23 (Tobi Corney). Photolibrary: cover and 15 (Botanica). Wayland Picture Library: 5, 7, 13, 21.

Library of Congress Cataloging-in-Publication Data

Edwards, Nicola.
Vegetables / Nicola Edwards. -- 1st ed.
p. cm. -- (See how plants grow)
Includes index.
ISBN-13: 978-1-4042-3700-1(library binding)
ISBN-10: 1-4042-3700-3 (library binding)
1. Vegetables--Juvenile literature. I. Title.
SB324.E39 2007
635--dc22
2006026531

Manufactured in China

Contents

What Are vegetables? 4

Where do vegetables grow? 6

Vegetables from different climates 8

Starting to grow 10

How plants make food 12

Food from roots 14

Food from stems 16

Food from leaves and flowers 18

How do we use vegetables? 20

Grow your own vegetables 22

Glossary 24

Index 24

Web Sites 24

What Are vegetables?

Vegetables are the parts of a plant that we eat–the leaves, **roots, stems,** and **flowers**. Vegetable plants grow throughout the year. Different vegetables are ready to eat in different seasons.

Some vegetables, such as carrots, grow under the ground.

A **fruit** is the part of a plant that contains **seeds**. You might think that foods, such as, peppers, green beans and zucchini, are vegetables, but they are actually fruits.

▼ Can you guess which of these are vegetables and which are fruits?

Where do vegetables grow?

Look around your local area to see if you can find vegetables growing. Some people have vegetable patches in their back yards where you might see asparagus, potatoes, spinach, or rhubarb.

▼ Some people grow their own vegetables to eat at home.

Visit a market or supermarket and look at the vegetables on display. Some may have been grown on farms nearby.

Vegetable Fact

Vegetables contain vitamins and fiber, which are important for us to eat to stay healthy.

The lettuce being planted on this farm will be sold in supermarkets.

Vegetables from different climates

Vegetables are grown all over the world, except near the freezing North and South Poles. Some vegetables such as yams, sweet potatoes, and taro are important vegetable crops in **tropical** regions.

These people are picking taro in Hawaii. People eat the taro's roots and leaves.

Others, such as lettuce, watercress, cabbage, and spinach, grow well in countries where the temperature is cooler. Vegetables, such as potatoes and onions, grow in countries that have warm summers and colder winters.

These onions are being picked in Northern Europe.

Starting to grow

Some vegetables, such as onions, begin life as a **bulb**. Others, such as radishes, grow from seeds. Both seeds and bulbs contain food for the plant that will develop from them. When a seed begins to grow, it is called **germination**.

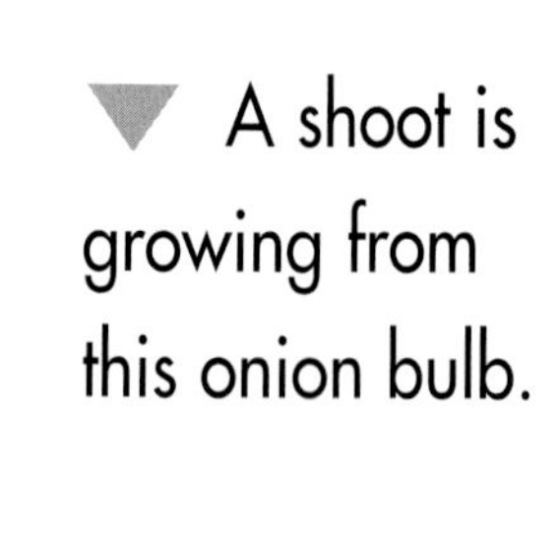

A shoot is growing from this onion bulb.

Roots grow down from the seed and a shoot grows upward from it, pushing through the ground toward the light.

The roots of these radishes take in water and **nutrients** from the soil.

How plants make food

Leaves grow from the stem of a vegetable plant. The stem holds the leaves up to the light. The leaves use light, water, and a gas called **carbon dioxide** from the air to make food for the plant.

▼ The leaves of plants contain **chlorophyll**, which makes them green.

Some vegetable plants, such as potatoes and yams, turn their food into a substance called **starch**, which fuels new growth.

▲ Eating starchy vegetables gives us **energy**.

Food from roots

Some of the vegetables we eat, such as carrots, beets, turnips, parsnips, radishes, and rutabaga, are the roots of plants. The part of the plant we eat is the main root, which grows larger than the other roots. This main root is called the **taproot**.

▼ These carrots are the main root of each carrot plant.

Vegetable Fact

Today's carrots are orange, but the world's first carrots were purple and yellow!

Root vegetables like these beets have to be dug up from the ground.

Food from stems

Some of the vegetables we eat are the stems of plants. Some stem vegetables, such as potatoes and yams, grow under the ground. The ginger plant looks like a tall grass above ground, but the part we eat is the thick underground stem. Other stem vegetables, such as rhubarb and celery, grow above the ground.

▼ Asparagus stems, sometimes called spears, have tiny leaves.

Vegetable Fact

Although we eat the stems of the rhubarb plant, its leaves are poisonous.

Ruby chard is a vegetable with red stems and green leaves.

Food from leaves and flowers

Some of the vegetables we eat are the leaves of plants. We call these leaf, or leafy, vegetables. Most leaf vegetables are green, but some types of spinach, cabbage, and salad leaves are red or purple.

▼ Leaf vegetables grow in a variety of shapes, sizes, and colors.

We eat the scented leaves of herb plants, such as mint, parsley, and coriander. Some vegetables, such as cauliflower and broccoli, are the plants' unopened flowers.

We eat the flower buds of the globe artichoke.

Vegetable Fact

Lettuce is named after the milky liquid it contains (from the French word for milk – *lait*).

How do we use vegetables?

We need to eat vitamin-rich vegetables to stay healthy. We eat some vegetables, such as carrots, celery, and spinach, raw in salads. There are many ways of cooking vegetables. They can be boiled, fried, roasted, steamed, and stewed.

▼ Vegetables are used to feed pets and farm animals.

Some vegetables such as onions and beets can be dried or pickled in vinegar. Medicines are made from vegetables, too.

This family eat tasty rice and vegetable dishes to keep themselves healthy.

Grow your own vegetables

See how a vegetable plant grows for yourself. Try growing lettuce from seeds. Fill a seed tray with some compost. Plant some seeds by pushing them gently into the compost until they are covered well. Water the compost, then put the tray in a warm, light place. How long does it take for your seed to grow?

Record what happens to your lettuce seeds.

▼ Plant the seedlings in some soil. Be sure to water them well.

Glossary

bulb
Some plants grow from a bulb. The bulb contains food for the plant.

carbon dioxide
A gas in the air that plants use to make food.

chlorophyll
A substance in leaves that helps make a plant's food. It also makes leaves green.

energy
What we need to help us move, work, and play.

fiber
A substance found in vegetables. It is an important part of a good diet.

flowers
The parts of some plants that have colorful petals.

fruit
The part of a plant that contains seeds.

germination
How a seed starts to develop into a plant.

leafy
Vegetables with leaves you can eat, like lettuce.

nutrients
Food in the soil that a plant needs for growth.

roots
The parts of a plant that hold it in the soil and take in water and nutrients.

seeds
Some plants grow from seeds.

starch
The substance a plant produces to give it energy for growth.

stem
The part of a plant that holds it upright. We eat some swollen underground stems, such as potatoes.

taproot
The main root of a plant that swells into the root vegetables we eat.

tropical
Areas of the world where it is hot and wet.

vitamins
Substances found in fruits and vegetables that we eat to keep us healthy.

Web Sites

Due to the changing nature of Internet links, PowerKids Press has developed an online list of Web sites related to the subject of this book. This site is regularly updated. Please use this link to access this list:
www.powerkidslinks.com/shpg/veg/

Index

animals 20
bulb 10
climate 8–9
farms 6–7
flowers 4, 19
food
  for the plants 10–11, 12–13
  from the plants 6, 14–19, 20–21
fruit 5
garden 6, 23
germination 10
healthy eating 6, 20–21
herbs 19
leaf vegetables 18–19
leaves 4, 8, 12, 16–17, 18–19
roots 4, 8, 10–11, 14
root vegetables 14–15
seasons 4
seeds 5, 10, 22
shoots 10
starch 13
stem 4, 12, 16–17
stem vegetables 16–17
taproot 14
underground vegetables 4, 14–15, 16
vitamins 6, 20
water 11, 12, 22–23